Kuroopa

Kuroopa

KAPIL RAJ

Anecdote
Publishing House

Anecdote Publishing House

E-35-A, E Block, Gali No. 2, Ganesh Nagar,
Pandav Nagar Complex, Delhi - 110092

Published by Anecdote Publishing House
Copyright © Kapil Raj

First Edition 2023

ISBN: 9788195890736

MRP: ₹ 149.00

Book Promoted and Marketed by Champ Readers Pvt. Ltd.

Layout and Cover by Anecdote
Printed in India

*To all the free souls,
hurt, chained, and caged
by social rules and
fabrications*

Change Stories by

Kapil Raj

Change Stories by Kapil Raj is an amalgamation of five independent short stories: ***Kuroopa, A Gutterful Life, First Love Many Times, Flying with Chains, and A Mother By The Window.***

Advancement of humankind invariably poses new challenges to the existing social order in society. It weakens the bondages enforced by patriarchal rules, paving the way for societal awakening. However, every ounce of progress leaves behind some debris in its wake. Failure to recognise this debris or 'problem' can bestow acute misery and suffering in the lives of people. Going back and snipping the problem in the bud is usually more cumbersome than revolting and moving forward.

If only there was an easy way out.

True social development cannot be achieved without breaking existing stereotypes and adapting our mindsets to the subsequent changes.

Each short story interweaves a heartening story with a deeply imbibed social issue, hardened public belief, and associated fabrications. As you read the narrative, you watch and evolve with the characters, sometimes feeling yourself in them – empathising in circumstances that may or may not have existed in your lives. The stories will highlight the suffering that was never supposed to take place had we brought about a meaningful change for ourselves and others in the society.

However, there's always a first, and it can start here.

We live how we think, and we think how we choose to live.
Progress is hard; change is heroic.

Acknowledgements

*E*very beginning has a story. We often emphasise too much on the journey and the end goal, forgetting all about that *first step*.

When I commenced writing *ENDURER A Rape Story*, I was scared spending nights on the outcome. From the inception of the idea to getting the story published, three years passed. The book finally, reached the hands of readers and found love in a way I had never imagined.

For the first time, when I held the mic in a room full of young students to speak on the subject (rape and sexual assaults) which is considered one of the biggest taboo in the Indian households, my hands trembled, yet I took that leap.

By the end of each of session, I was gifted emotions, witnessed appreciation and respect. It was a dream come true. But a thought lingered behind. What next? What topic should I pick? Will I be able to justify the appreciation and recognition I received? The turmoil was too much. For a moment, I felt giving up. In those times, there are people who stand with you, influencing in ways which do not let yourself stop and take on unfamiliar paths.

They are my parents, my wife Payal, my sister Dimple and my son Hetarth. I owe you.

Pulkit, Thank You. You always stood along. When I simply could not progress further, your faith in me made me hold on and continue to move.

Tatiana, I am grateful for your persuasion and astute conversations. You incepted ideas on which I was able to write and build these stories.

Tina, you have my gratitude. You chiselled out the entire work with your editing and added a clear voice to the words.

Sincere thanks to Anecdote Publishers & Sagar Azad, who trusted me with my unconventional project and extended all support to get published.

And most importantly, I would like to thank all my readers. Your reviews, personal texts, praises and critiques motivated me to walk through this journey.

1

*Pooja, work on your daughter's behaviour. It was our mistake to invite Meera for the birthday party. The girl has turned the entire celebration into a disaster." Mrs Gulati's voice echoed from the speaker.

Pooja was speechless and had no clue how to respond. Usually, a mother would lambaste the protester, but this was about Meera.

"I am telling you, because of this girl, the lamp that had to be lit as part of the prayer, diffused. If anything bad happens… I am just saying… this girl is responsible, such a *kali chaya* (dark aura)," she said, continuing to curse when Mr Gulati interrupted and snatched the receiver.

"Don't mind her, Mrs Sharma. She is a little upset. You know her, all her senses go for a toss when she is angry. Just ask Meera to be careful in the future; we wish her the best."

"I will. Thank you, Gulati Ji."

Pooja had no guts to ask what Meera had done. She put the receiver down with tears. It was not the incident but her fears coming true in ways worse than she had imagined. The age difference between her daughters, Ashna and Meera was just one year. They were fruits of the same branch, but their appearances disharmonized, unlike any other siblings.

Ashna was the elder and pretty one – a well-defined nose, clear complexion, rosebud lips, and a unique bluish tint in her eyes acquired from her grandfather's side. On the other hand, Meera had an extremely thick nose as if moulded at birth, a dark complexion, a tiny forehead, a broad chin, and was slightly overweight. Pooja loved her children equally but there was no denying that Ashna always got a little extra attention wherever they went. Whenever they visited their relatives, there was always a never-ending commentary of 'Oh! They are sisters?' '*Arey*, what happened to this one?' 'What did you eat before this one?' 'What did you look at when she was inside you?' The worst one was from her mother-in-law – 'Bahu, conceive one more time and do what I tell you. You will have a beautiful boy who looks just like Ashna.' And she did. Deven, miraculously, looked just like Ashna.

She was jolted out of her reverie by the sound of

the main gate. Both her daughters entered with their heads down. Meera tried to walk past her, but Pooja grabbed her arm angrily. First the atrocious behaviour and then she had the gall to misbehave at home too! Pooja was furious. But when she saw the panic and terror in Meera's eyes, she let go of her daughter's hand. Meera scuttled away like a fish released into the water.

"What happened?" Pooja asked Ashna.

"At first, she was not participating in the games. Then the kids started teasing her that she was adopted and exchanged in the hospital."

"And how did you help your sister when all this was going on?"

"I told them to stop. Instead, she slapped me and pushed the other kids – they fell on the cake. One of the boys reciprocated, but she threw a glass of juice at him, that landed on the floor of the nearby temple area."

"Where were the elders?"

"They were busy; it was a huge gathering. All of this happened in a matter of minutes."

Ashna started weeping. Pooja switched on the television to divert their mind and moved to the channel playing their favourite show.

At night, Pooja quietly checked on her children. Ashna and Deven were fast asleep. Meera was lying on her side. With her experienced hands, Pooja directly touched Meera's eyelashes and understood. Her act of fake sleeping and wiping her cheeks did not work. She gathered Meera in her arms and hugged her. A stream of tears flowed from her daughter's eyes.

"Mummy, are you angry with me?" she asked.

"No."

"Mummy, you say Sai Baba is fair to all. Then why did he make me so ugly? Am I not your daughter? Was I exchanged at the hospital? Or did you leave me in the sun one day and that's why I became so dark?"

Pooja's heart melted on hearing such words from her daughter. She was in the sixth grade – all this negativity could have a profound impact on her future. She released Meera and made her sit comfortably. Holding her chin up, she said, "You are my daughter, and I love you more than myself. Sai Baba will guide us towards our destiny. Looks don't matter. When you grow up, you'll realise that the heart is the most important thing in life. Remember this."

2

As we grow up, some incidents from our past, a few words spoken in particular circumstances, form the basis of our beliefs and understanding of this world. When those beliefs shatter for any reason, our entire journey of self-realisation comes to a standstill and scars the person in many ways.

There is a fine line between truth and falsehood. A line that is regularly trod by many. When Pooja said 'looks don't matter,' she believed it was true. Even today, the answer would be the same if someone ask her. This statement gets much more support in books, movies, and general conversations, so the scale generally seems to tip towards the truth. But in reality, this truth is nothing but a lie – get it?

If looks don't matter, then why does the billion-dollar cosmetic industry exist? Or why do we have beauty pageants? Why are filters available on social media platforms to improve our face? Why are the protagonists of movies well-built and chiselled actors?

Pooja was an educated girl from a small town. She knew her fate after college – marriage. In smaller cities, marriage is a marketplace, there are no 'made in heaven' matches – another 'lie', but we will return to this later. One knows what they are going to get. Education, financial status, caste, religion, ancestral relationships, diseases, health, background, etc., are some of the main factors that decide a person's prospects. However, two criteria can override all the other factors –

money and looks. If one is specially-abled but has a hefty dowry, they can still find a match in a good family. Or if one is exceptionally beautiful but has no financial level, they too have the potential to marry above their status.

Pooja was able to become the *bahu* of the *haveli* because of this criterion only. Mr Sharma was shy, well-built, and extremely dark. The local marriage counsellors and pandits were asked to look for one thing – find a girl of the same religion and caste, but she should be extremely pretty and fair. They asked for zero gifts and dowry. When Pooja met her mother-in-law for the first time, her cheeks were stretched and pulled. Her mother-in-law peered through her thick glasses to check if what she had heard was true – 'white as snow' the girl is, they said. The town was swept with disbelief when they heard that Sharmaji took no dowry for his last son. The marriages of the other three brothers were expensive market deals and business relationships.

Later, Mr Sharma got a government job and relocated to the city. The family moved with him. It took some time for Pooja to adjust to her new surroundings, but her education helped in settling down. Years had passed since this phase of her life, which is why it was easy for her to forget and say 'looks don't matter.' At best, with her family's status, she could have married a decent shopkeeper or an employee at a local showroom. But she married into the wealthiest family of her town only because of her looks.

No, destiny could have done nothing if she wasn't fair enough.

3

❦

"*I* won," said Ashna, entering the home with a trophy and a certificate. Her voice was brimming with pride. The chief guest who judged the inter-school debate competition remarked that Ashna had 'exceptional potential.'

She had practised tirelessly for many nights, but in the end, her presence of mind, confidence, and commanding voice worked in her favour. Mr Sharma put the newspaper aside and appreciated the trophy. He placed his hand on Ashna's head and looked at her for a while. His eyes were blank and lost in tides of thought. He zoned back in, smiled at her, and gave her a two thousand rupee note from his pocket.

He called Meera and Deven, who stood behind Ashna.

"There is no win without participation," he said, addressing his younger children and gifting them with some money as well.

The kids accepted the cash from their father and went to their rooms. Deven was overjoyed; he knew what we wanted to buy – a new Transformer toy. All he did was drag a few crayons on a white sheet of paper in the drawing competition. Meera quietly walked to her table and stashed the money in a box. She had worked hard on her essay for the competition. It was lost among the average ones, she figured. Rereading her notes, she tore them apart, eyes wet with tears.

Her door flew open; she quickly wiped her eyes. Ashna came in and fell on the bed. Meera glanced at her. She saw a winner, unconsciously expressing her potential as if she was born for it. Ashna excelled at everything. A class topper, captain of the school basketball team, and a terrific dancer. After getting bored of her other accomplishments, she tried for the debate team that year. As expected, she defeated students from all the top schools. In Meera's opinion, the other participant had done really well and could have won, but the last-minute aggression by Ashna, with a shaking head, bulging eyes, sweat visible on her marble skin, and the firmness in her voice, tipped the balance in her favour. How beautiful Ashna looked at that moment. Like a princess demanding her throne, she stood against all the kingdoms and made them kneel before her.

Meera noticed that Ashna was smiling; maybe

she was visualising her winning moment. She observed and compared herself to her sister every day. Ashna's presence made her speechless, not worthy of existence. Instead of catching up, she was falling apart. She recalled dad's expression when he placed his hand on Ashna's head. A pure sense of relief, a wave of pride, something that makes one happy right to their inner core. Dad never laughed, but she read it in his eyes. Maybe in this life, she could get the same response from her dad, but the possibility was slim with Ashna around. Not even average – she was nothing but a failure.

The local news had various photos of the inter-school competition and a separate column dedicated to the winners. Ashna's face was all over the papers. Dad folded the newspaper and put it in his bag before leaving for the office. Their relatives called, and neighbours dropped in during the day to congratulate them. Ashna was greeted like a celebrity at school – there was no limit to her fame. The higher Ashna rose, the deeper Meera sank with an invisible weight.

4

*A*shna sailed through to 12th grade, the last level of schooling, and was geared up to prepare for the board exams. Her aim was to qualify for the top colleges of Delhi University, for which she needed top grades. All the colleges in their town were archaic, with no possibility of the fancy campus life she wanted – one that we saw in movies or TV shows. She thought she was too good to spend her life in the city. Before settling, she wanted to experience the world, get the best education, and build a career.

On the other hand, Meera was struggling even to clear her exams. Her obsession with Ashna was getting out of control. She would sit in front of her books for hours, staring at them blankly and imagining a life where there was no comparison with her sister. A world where her physical flaws were not considered ugly and where people were happy to see her. She would dream that her appearance was magically replaced with Ashna's, and the impact it would have on her daily life. Eventually, she realised that Ashna would leave the next year and she would struggle to even get into a decent college in the city. Her sleep pattern got disturbed, which in turn impacted her diet – she started eating all the time.

To improve her grades, Meera joined tuition classes for the complicated subjects. Nothing changed. Instead of focusing on the teacher, her thoughts would wander towards the other kids of the batch who were ignoring her presence completely. For the first few days, when she reached early, she sat on one side of the last bench. After a while, no one sat on that seat, even when the class was almost full. Oh, there sits a weird girl. Do not occupy that seat! Such excessive thoughts hindered her concentration on academics.

So when a boy gently shook her hand one day, asking her how she was, she was shocked and completely out of words. The best she could do was to nod and say, 'Thank you.' She spent the entire night pondering on her idiotic response. There was no doubt that the boy would never talk to her again. She deserved to be ignored by people. But when he initiated a conversation again, a tiny smile emerged on her face.

His name was Kushal, and after the class, he introduced her to his group. She recognised many of them and was surprised that they were okay to talk to her now. Coming from a different school, she enjoyed their gossip and conversations. She remained silent most of the time, trying her best not to say something stupid and become a joke like she was for her classmates.

"We are going to a pizza place tomorrow after class. Would you like to come?" asked Kushal.

Meera stared at him in disbelief. An invitation for an outing? She hid her happiness and nodded joyfully, giving her consent. On the way home, she debated what she would wear, how she would speak or reply to questions, thinking about in a loop. But first she needed permission from her mother.

Pooja was busy cooking in the kitchen and didn't even notice Meera creeping up behind her. She stood with her hands clasped in a dove position, feet tapping the floor. Meera was afraid to say anything.

"What is it, *beta*?"

"Mom, can I come home a little late after tuitions tomorrow?"

"Why?" questioned Pooja, surprised at this request.
As if she had committed a crime, Meera told Pooja about her plan with friends in a small voice.

Pooja looked at her daughter and smiled in her heart. She remembered when Ashna had come to her for permission to go out for the first time a few years ago. Yes, Meera was late by many years, but better late than never. It was still a positive sign. Pooja hid her joy and nodded, quietly handing over some money from her purse.

"Just get back before dad comes home."

5

That night, Meera's mind sprinted at the speed of light. She remembered falling asleep for a few hours below sunrise. Then the dreams haunted her again – the inevitable fear of how she would become a laughing stock in front of others. The following day, she sat through school with a splitting headache. She even got a scolding from one of the teachers for her inattentiveness. After school was over, finally it was time to get ready for the tuition class. She could feel her heart pounding in her chest.

For a moment, she thought of skipping the class by calling in sick. Yes, that was the best thing to do – avoid the situation before it turns into anything worse. She was still debating what to do when Pooja knocked on her door.

"You are not ready yet?"

"I'm not feeling well, mom."

Pooja saw through the hesitancy, her fear clearly. Meera was quite old, but she had never had a friend. Unlike Ashna, she never spoke about her school life. It was as if it didn't exist. Meera was circling in a dead zone of her fancies.

"At times, you must break the barriers around you to see what's on the other side, Meera. Try to meet people, expand your circle. Fear exists only in your head. Don't be afraid. Everything will be fine; I have full faith in you."

No, she didn't. These are the instances when lies are necessary. One should not take truths and lies so literally. Morals are being defined constantly; they are being created as weapons of heaven and hell. Both are a simple part of speech and are meant for progress. The core of the matter lies in the intention behind it.

Meera did not know this. Most of us drift in these "word storms" and get completely entangled in our lives. For some time, Meera thanked her mother in her heart. After the tuition class, they rode their scooters and bikes to a pizza place nearby. Kushal offered to order the speciality for everyone, including Meera. People who have conquered the art of social interaction – naturally or through repeated efforts, have no idea of the impact their tiny acts make on others. Kushal ensured Meera's comfort despite her initial hesitancy. She swarmed with happiness in return; she felt so light that she could fly at any moment. Meera was finally part of a group that valued her presence, and Kushal had made it happen. They chatted, made jokes, mimicked teachers, clicked photos, and uploaded them on Facebook. When it was time to leave, Meera walked up to Kushal.

"Thank you for this."

"Oh, no need. You are so sweet," he said and in an instant, patted her head, laughing.

A wave of shock went through Meera. She controlled her feelings and went home, thinking about the happiest evening of her life. Pooja waited for her, praying that everything went well, and when Meera entered with a smile and no puffy eyes, she uttered a sigh of relief.

In school, Meera kept thinking about her small outing. She eagerly waited for the day to pass and her tuition class to arrive. When getting ready, she looked at herself in the mirror for a while. After some thinking, she opened the dressing drawer and picked Ashna's comb. Instead of the usual ponytail, she let her hair hang loose and braided two tiny branches like Ashna, then she cinched them with a butterfly clip at the back of her head, leaving the rest of her hair to fall free. She secretly watched her sister making different hairstyles and was surprised to recall every move.

When she passed through the living room, Ashna and Pooja looked at each other and smiled. Meera noticed and blushed. Feeling embarrassed, she walked quickly and escaped the house.

"Finally," said Ashna, and Pooja agreed with her daughter.

Meera reached the venue and parked her scooter next to the others. She uncovered her face and locked the helmet. No one said anything, but she noticed other girls observing her new hairstyle. She felt thrilled. They chatted for a while before the class started. After it ended, they continued to talk when Kushal asked Meera to come aside for a bit – he wanted to ask her something.

"You look different today," he said.

"Really? I don't know. Good or bad?"

"Good, obviously. Well, I have a tiny favour to ask from you."

"Tell me. I don't know how I can be of any help to anyone," replied Meera, blushing slightly.

"You are so humble. Ashna Sharma is your sister, right?"

Meera's excitement, the tiny speck of confidence, plummeted instantly after hearing Ashna's name. She got a hint about where this was going. She prayed to Sai Baba that her intuition was wrong. Please God, not this time.

"Ya, yes. What about her?" said Meera, her face turning into plastic.

"Can you… I mean," he hesitated a little. "Can you introduce me to her? You know, I saw her debate, and it was like –"

In that moment, if someone had pierced Meera's skin with a needle, she would have failed to notice. Such was the impact of Kushal's deception. She lowered her head, turned, and sprinted towards her scooter. She left the premises as fast as she could, leaving Kushal and the group wondering. On reaching home, Meera rushed to the bathroom locking herself in. Undoing her hair angrily, she yelled silently and started to weep uncontrollably.

This was not the first time this has happened. Boys would occasionally approach her so they could connect with Ashna. It was part of growing up, and she had stopped minding this a long time ago. But such betrayal from a person she thought was a friend… just to get to Ashna! It was unbearable. For once she felt like she was part of a group. She thought they actually liked her and valued her – it was nothing but a sham. Being Ashna's sister was nothing but a curse. How was she ever going to get rid of it? She lay down on the bed and sandwiched her head between two pillows. This way, nobody would know if she was asleep or awake, and she could cry as much as she wanted. That was the last day she went to the tuition class.

6

❦

$\mathcal{P}$ooja's worry for Meera mounted with the passing years. She watched her daughter suffocating inside, repressing her feelings every single day. No one can regulate the interaction of their children with the outside world. Her inability to control or make things better was even worse. She was not surprised when Meera ran, hiding her face after a day of her supposedly great pizza outing. Sensing a vibe, she sneaked into the kid's room after some time. Meera was lying on her side with her face sandwiched between two pillows.

Pooja knew Meera was crying – this was her secret way of doing it, thinking nobody would know. But it was Pooja who picked the pillow from the floor when Meera fell asleep. Today was the first time she had seen her daughter dress happily for an occasion, only to return feeling miserable as ever. For sure, Meera had gone through a terrible incident. Pooja's prayers for Meera's successful adventure did not work.

Few months later, they visited one of the popular designer stores to shop clothes for Diwali. The sales boys flitted around Ashna, suggesting the best designs that would look great on her. Meera observed all this in silence, coyly trying the outfits rejected by Ashna. She softly asked about the availability of a large size. At first, her request went unheard. When Ashna was done choosing her outfit, one of the staff members turned to Meera and showed her three or four options.

"These are so bad. Don't you have anything

better?" asked Meera, frustratingly.

"Ma'am, we have the best items in the city. But sizes are not available for all styles," he replied, smirking at Meera.

Overhearing the conversation, Pooja barged in and threw the dresses at the attendant's face.

"Then what is the point of being the best in the market? Scoundrel, how dare you speak about my daughter's size? Look at yourself… as if your mother has not fed you in a month!"

Hearing the commotion, the manager came rushing towards them.

"Educate your staff if you need loyal customers!" yelled Pooja and dragged Meera out of the store. She had almost stepped out when Ashna stopped her; she pleaded with her eyes.

"Mom, I love that dress… it is so cheap here," she said in a muffled voice.

"We will find it somewhere else," replied Pooja. "But mom…"

"Follow me," said Pooja, giving the final ultimatum. No request was entertained after this; only the order was followed.

The manager kept apologising, but Pooja left, taking her girls with her. Ashna crossed her arms and reluctantly followed her mother and sister, muttering under her breath on their way out. They tried other showrooms, but Ashna's heart was set on that selected piece. With one girl fuming and the other lolling about in silence, Pooja called it a day and returned home empty-handed. This was the worst thing that could happen, going shopping but coming back empty-handed – such a waste of time.

"Mom, you overreacted at the shop," said Ashna, breaking the silence as Pooja prepared the evening tea.

"That boy disrespected –"

"Don't you think, for once, that he was not wrong in his place?" She interrupted her mother and turned towards Meera. "Sis, I am not your enemy. I'm sorry to break this to you, but lose this flab for everyone's sake. It is not healthy at all."

"Ashna, stop it!" warned Pooja.

"Why, mom? You are not doing her any favours by keeping her away from reality. What is wrong with speaking the truth?"

"So now you will teach your mother?"

"Everyone makes fun of her. Do you like that? I never say it, but many times it's because of me that she is spared for her weird behaviour."

Pooja stared at her daughter. What was going on? Had she grown up so much to disrespect her mother?

"But now people have started asking me why I don't do anything about it. What should I say… that my mom spoils her? She has become a pumpkin, but my mother has become blind in her love for her. I don't understand why you appreciate this dumb behaviour. She does not participate in any activities or does well in her studies. What does she even do all the time except eat like there is no tomorrow?" Ashna went on and on.

"Last week, she almost burned down the chemistry lab. A month before, the principal herself caught her cheating on a test! She spoiled the entire decoration in the class fest by tripping over it. I mean, how retarded can one be to behave this way? How could…"

Meera finally gave in and broke down, covering her face. Everything became muffled around her. What those tears were for, she did not know. Home is synonymous with support and solace. Ashna had never attacked her like this before. She was always very busy thriving in her world and had no time to interfere in her sister's life. What happened to her today? That day, Ashna gave voice to her fears and doubts. She had to clear the air once and for all.

"Yes, start weeping now. Victimise yourself. That's the only thing you are good at. But remember, the world doesn't give a damn about cry-babies. But we are family, so I will shut up."

"One more word Ashna, and you will be grounded for a week!" said Pooja, her voice quivering with anger. Her mother's quaking hands made Ashna back off. The right to speak and present your thoughts is overrated. How about understanding the effect on the listener? No, we never talk about that. We preach freedom of speech and claim not to hear anyone except our hearts. Is anyone ever going to decode these strange parallels?

Pooja understood every word that came out of Ashna's mouth. She always hoped that things would improve in the future. They never do, at least by thinking. She glanced at both of her daughters. One, ready to take on the world on her terms, and the other, waiting to be devoured by it. Where did she go wrong? Was her upbringing to blame? Or is the harsh reality that standards of physical attributes can impact one's life to a great extent actually true?

7

❧

*M*eera collapsed on the balcony, silently whimpering for comfort. No questions, no judgement, just a plain stream of pain, no effort to even stop, no question behind the reason as well. Lying on the floor, chin resting on her arm, she stretched two fingers inside the cage of two parakeets – Tutti and Frutti. They were Ashna's birds, used as props in many of her videos on Instagram. The birds trusted Meera and settled on her fingers whenever she inserted them inside their home. It was an unusual empowering bond.

The birds did not look down at her for being obese, dark, or weird.

Ashna's words tore through her soul and resonated endlessly. She was such a dead weight on everyone, a living disgrace. She wished she was never born. God sprinkles a little pain in everyone's lives to balance the blessings irrespective of being rich or poor. She was that imperfection for her almost seamless family. Things would be better if she simply vanished or died.

This sudden idea gave her jitters, and she turned to face the sky. A pang of hunger interrupted her musings. The thoughts of taking her life and devouring a snack thrust her into a bout of self-humiliation and disgust for her body. She slapped herself. The rising hatred inside her increased her desire for food even further.

While Meera contemplated, Deven entered the room with his usual bang – he always shoved the door a bit harder than required. The unexpected thump sounded like an explosion to the little birds, terrifying them. The fingers they rested on retreated to cover the face of their owner so that the tears could remain hidden from the world. With the cage door open and unattended, Tutti exited his prison to witness the outside world. He landed on the edge of the balcony. Frutti quickly followed in her partner's steps. Chirping gleefully, the birds spread their wings and leaped from the balcony with their limited understanding. Their flapping brought Meera back to her senses and she rolled around – the birds had escaped. Meera jumped up in shock and witnessed their flight to freedom. Two tiny innocent life-forms vanished amid the concrete jungle.

Deven slapped his forehead and screeched. Panic-stricken, he watched Meera turn, equally terrified. They both were imagining how Ashna would react, but they did not need to wait for long to find out. First, the missed dress, and then the conflict with their mother – Ashna's mood was thoroughly spoiled already. She knew she wouldn't be able to focus on anything, however hard she tried. So she decided to go to her friend's place on the pretext of studying, but she would listen to music and watch TV to calm herself.

Deven's face turned pale and sweaty while Meera sat on the balcony floor with her head down. Finding a weepy Meera was usual, but Deven? Ashna walked over to the almirah, wondering. She placed her lacy violet top and blue jeans on the bed. She picked a book as a prop for the study session and suddenly noticed the cage lying on the floor – it was usually hung by a hook next to the door. It was empty – the tragedy hit her like a brick.

She threw the book aside and marched towards Meera, bursting with rage.

"Who left the cage open!" she yelled.

Meera's lips quivered in fear.

"Meera, I swear, your useless tears do not work on me. Tell me right now, who did this?"

"I… I…"
Having the entire day ruined by Meera, Ashna could not control her anger anymore and she punched Meera on the shoulder.

"You idiot! Is this your creepy way of taking revenge? How low can you stoop?"

"I will find them," stuttered Meera.

"You killed them, do you get it? They are house-bred birds. They can barely fly for a minute. Poor souls have no sense of direction or skills to find food or water. They will die of hunger or fear… even worse, get eaten by predators like cats or dogs. Do you feel happy now? For getting back at your sister for speaking the truth?"

Meera looked up, pleading with Ashna to understand her younger sister. Why would she mind being called weird or unfit when she had been hearing this since childhood? Yes, she was broken and hurt, but Ashna was her idol, and today even she had humiliated her. All the disgrace she had accumulated throughout her life would have vanished had she achieved even an iota of success when compared to Ashna.

Ashna did not understand her sister; she never cared to listen.

"I will not forgive you for this," said Ashna, grabbing her clothes and storming out of the room.

8

*A*fraid and distressed, Deven narrated the entire incident to Pooja. She continued to wash and chop the vegetables while her heart exploded. Pooja offered him his favourite chocolate bar and sent him to play at a friend's house. After shutting the gate, she walked in and sat in the temple area.

"Why did you make my daughter ugly?" Yes, she said it, with no denial. It would have been better if all her children looked alike. Meera had inherited the worst features from them. Things are not that difficult for a solo child as they don't have to face the brunt of comparison in their homes – it's their safe haven. But for her Meera, every day was torture. As a child, she endured judgement, and as a teenager, things were becoming even more traumatic day by day. She knew for a fact that her soft-hearted child had been the fulcrum of problems in the house for many years. Breaking glass, forgetting things after purchasing them, getting late when it was important to be on time – she always heard back from Deven and Ashna. At times, Pooja felt that Meera had given up all hope.

This time, she was out of ideas on how to calm Meera. She quickly prepared the food and rushed towards her daughter's room. She peered inside; the beds were empty. Hearing the sound of the balcony fan, she walked outside. Meera sat on the floor, muttering under her breath. The empty cage lay on her lap.

"… honestly. I am sorry. I repeat this for the

millionth time. I am not your murderer. Our souls are connected. I hear from you. And maybe when I die, which will be soon, we will meet at the door of heaven. Because I don't know if they will allow me there, but you will definitely have your place. But I want to see you one last time. I am sorry –" her voice broke as she sucked in air between sobs.

"I am not a bad person. I know I always disappoint people, despite wanting everyone's happiness. I can only wish but not give – how can I? One can only give something they have, right Tutti, Frutti? Can you answer me? You can't... you are gone."

Pooja fell against the wall, clutching the mantle and stifling her mouth from screaming. But she wanted to hear, no matter how much those words pierced her soul. Meera continued as if she was alone in the world, and only the empty cage existed with her.

"Teachers compare me with Ashna, aunties tell

me to behave like a girl. Speak more, else I won't get married. Who will like a dark-complexioned fatty like me, anyway? No looks, no brain, and no attitude. I know I will die alone, but you knew this too. Then why did you leave? Answer me, or were you tired of me as well?"

"Meera!" yelled Pooja, unable to control herself anymore. However, Meera did not respond, as if the words did not reach her.

"I had hopes that one day I will make my mommy proud, I will make my dad smile like he does for Ashna, but I am giving up, every single day... little by little. I will..."

Pooja gripped her shoulders from behind, trying to make Meera sit but instead, she fell in her lap. Noticing her face, Pooja screamed in shock. Meera's eyes were bloodshot, her body was shaking, and she was completely drenched in sweat.

"… world has no place for me. Such an ugly disgrace…" continued Meera.

Pooja held her arms and shook her. When there was no change, she gently slapped her cheeks.

"Mother, are you here? Mother, I am a burden on you. But I promise…"

"Wake up, Meera!" screamed Pooja, embracing her, but Meera kept blubbering without pausing. With all her might, Pooja picked her up and dragged her to bed. She lay next to her and murmured prayer's in her ears. It was a while before Meera gave up and finally went to sleep.

Pooja instructed Ashna and Deven to use the guest room that night and obstructed Mr Sharma's view of the television – she wanted to catch his attention. Rightfully aggravated, he maintained his calm, noticing the expression on his wife's face.

"Listen to me, Sharmaji. You have been ignorant for long enough. See a doctor, therapist, change the house, city, separate these girls, but take charge of Meera," said Pooja.

Maintaining his silence, he understood that something grave had transpired. He inquired with a shake of his head. Pooja narrated the incident, but Mr Sharma's expression remained platonic.

"Please say something. Tell me it is going to be ok!" pleaded Pooja.

"Only Meera can decide this," he said and went back to watching his show.

9

The following day was a Sunday. Before sleeping, Mr Sharma asked Pooja to check if Meera could get up early and join him. Mr Sharma went to the temple every Sunday for a few hours of solace. This request was a significant step from his side as he had never asked any of his children to join him. Pooja was slightly relieved when she heard this. She chanted Sai Baba's hymns the entire night, patting Meera's head gently. She believed the vibrations from her songs would have a calming effect on her daughter. Meera woke up in the middle of the night and was surprised to find herself wrapped in her mother's arms. Pooja rushed to the kitchen, made her something to eat, and then enveloped her in her arms again. They wept together without speaking. Their silence spoke the language of love. Almost in a trance, Meera could not resist the warmth of her mother's embrace and let herself sink in the depths of the night.

#

The car stopped at the temple gate. Meera was still reeling under the aftermath of last night's events, but she was used to this by now. She occasionally pressed her temple to ease the headache. It did not abate as her mind was still racing to understand the reason behind this outing. It was a fact that dad visited the temple every Sunday and returned around noon. Why did he ask her to join him? He always went alone. Was he also fed up with her after the Tutti-Frutti incident and wanted to scold her? Her father's expressions were blank so she couldn't figure this out by simply looking at his face.

They walked up the stairs and entered the main complex. Few people greeted Mr Sharma along the way and he replied with a nod. A magnificent idol of Goddess Kali stood in all its glory in front of them. It was surrounded by people. Instead of getting close and taking blessings from the priest, Mr Sharma settled on the glassy marble with an unobstructed view of the deity. He closed his eyes and clasped his hands to his chest. The world vanished around him and it was time for the Goddess to convene with her devotee. Meera followed her dad, but lost her concentration in a few seconds. She looked around – carved pillars, trees at a distance, people lost in their devotion, singing songs, and dancing to the temple bells. So many wishes and aspirations, who was going to listen to them? Suddenly, she felt something piercing through her soul. It seemed Goddess Kali had spotted her, sitting in her abode and doubting the strength of the master and the dedication of other people. Meera immediately apologised and looked up at her. She saw the startling image of a woman with four hands holding a blood smeared dagger, a severed man's head, and a bowl that collected the dripping blood. She wore a necklace of human skulls and a skirt made of human arms. With her red eyes, lolling tongue, unkempt hair and dark appearance, Goddess Kali's representation was unique compared to the images of other Gods Meera had seen.

For no reason, Meera's breath escalated and a tear fell out, acknowledging the beauty of Goddess Kali. The general image was not new to her, but for the first time, she processed this embodiment. Yes, she did not find it fearful. Instead, she sensed protection. That *maa* would demolish her inner demons and eradicate fear from the world. She could just be, if only for a moment. Whether her prayers would be heard or not, she felt empowered that the people obsessed with fair skin and beauty bow to this magnificent individual, begging for their wishes to come true.

Meera was so engrossed in her thoughts that she completely lost track of time. Suddenly she noticed her father waiting for her. She immediately nodded and both of them got up. They finally went near the idol, bowed their heads, and took blessings from the priest.

#

Confused between fear, excitement and doubt, Meera knew this was not it. They were hours away from noon, and the road taken was not for their home. She forgot her headache and kept trying to figure out the reason her dad had brought her along. Still, not a word or expression on Mr Sharma's face.

The car stopped in front of an ancient building. The rusty, corroded name plate was not legible at first sight. Instead of hanging on the wall or above the gate, the small square was mounted on a plinth in the ground. The security guard's body obstructed half of the name, but still, Meera could figure out from the legible words that it was a home for mentally disabled children.

The guard saluted Mr Sharma with a smile; his eyes were fixated on Meera. She bobbed her head like her dad. Dried yellow bushes protruded from the ground over a brick walkway, and the garden was nothing but a lifeless land. Meera sensed this was part of dad's ritual – may have been for years – which he never shared with the family.

They walked in through a half-open wooden door. There was a massive hallway with doors lined up on the side. It seemed to connect with a series of corridors with an open area in the centre. Considering the barren landscape outside the premises, the atmosphere inside was drastically different because of all the lighting, sounds, and irregular shrieks. A young boy appeared in the hallway, screaming and running with disoriented steps. A staff member followed him with an injection in his hand, clearly frustrated. He called out the boy's name, but it had no impact. The man leaped and caught the boy by his shirt. First, he placed the injection in his pocket and then, with the second arm, caught the boy's neck and made him walk with a bit of force.

"What is the matter?" An older adult with a balding head, wearing a white coat, yelled out. Meera quickly identified him as the doctor.

"Sir, Gopi again," screamed the nurse, taking the boy to one of the rooms.

The doctor scratched his shiny dome as if thinking about the medication for Gopi. But when his eyes fell on Mr Sharma, he forgot everything and rushed to greet him.

"Good morning Sharma Ji!" said the doctor, eyeing Meera. "How are your studies beta? I've asked your father to visit with his family so many times, but you know him," he said, shrieking with laughter at his remark. Meera wondered if her father had ever mentioned this place, but she couldn't recall. She smiled back just like her dad.

"Come, Rawat Ji is waiting for you." The trio walked along the corridor while Meera scanned her surroundings. The doctor had to leave them mid-way as one of the patients needed his attention. Mr Sharma continued to walk with his head raised, exchanging greetings in signs. She was baffled to see how people understood and followed her father's silent language. Through a series of turns, they entered a vast room. A burst of smell hit her nostrils and Meera understood they were entering a kitchen. The cooks beamed when they saw them.

Shortly, a seeming manager walked in and greeted Sharma Ji.

"Everything is in order, sir," he said, smiling with respect and gratitude.

Sharma Ji replied by pointing at the sky, indicating God. Together, they inspected the food items that were ready to be served for breakfast and then the ones prepared for lunch – dal, mixed veg, kheer, roti, poori and rice. The kitchen was connected to the dining hall, and right before the serving gate there was a huge pane of glass separating the two sections. Meera could see half-eaten plates of food before the children who were seated on long dining tables. Few of them were physically adults but still had a child's mind. These were the ones who sat by themselves while a nurse or attendant accompanied everyone else. Many of them needed help just to hold the spoon. They would make an effort to look at the plate, pick the food, and then chew it slowly. She was sure many would not understand that there was something special about the meal, or maybe they would, but that is not the point.

The bodies of the children vanished; her view began to glaze over. Definitions and beliefs started to question their existence. Meera had looked up to Ashna every single day of her life. She wanted to be liked, loved, have friends, and be appreciated by the people around her. Now, she could identify a fundamental flaw in her dream. It was too self-centred. She was too focused on what she did not have instead of recognising what she did. These kids may not be fighters, but they held the line. A child beamed as her tongue sensed the sweet taste of dessert. She was clapping, nodding her head, and shaking with joy. She was more open to happiness than Meera ever was.

Overwhelmed by a surge of emotions, Meera reeled on the spot and fell. She cried and cried. She thought she was the most miserable person on Earth, that the world and God had been unjust to her. She blamed everyone, her sister, mother, and classmates, but the truth is, each life is different. Everyone has their own story and share of grief.

Those children brought her back to reality. Life is not just about yourself; it cannot be. The entire living species, their existence, is connected with each other. Meera was incredibly privileged to have such a well-maintained family. She had a roof, a strong father, a caring mother, siblings, food to eat, and most importantly, a healthy mind and a fully working body. Yes, she weighed four times the usual, but that was just temporary. The truth is always there; we just refuse to acknowledge it. Controlling her impulses and taking responsibility for her body was her job alone.

Meera wiped her tears and got up with some help from her father. She looked at the children once more. She was not ready to face them today, but she vowed to return.

"Let's go."

10

Mr. Sharma glanced at his daughter. He sensed she was ready, and now she was leaving, just like he had once. He had a smile on his face, the unique one that Meera was fond of. She was surprised to see it because she had done nothing except break down in front of the staff. Moreover, Ashna was also not around. So who was it for?

"Dad, why was there an old photo of you along with our uncles and grandfather in the main hall?"

Mr Sharma's smile widened. Finally, he spoke.

"You have a unique ability to notice things. Even your mother missed it when I brought her here," he replied. "This was our land. We donated it to the government to build the institution."

"Do our uncles ever come here?" asked Meera.

"No, they don't. They don't have the time or need. There is so much to do in town."

They walked back to the car. Meera closed her eyes and rode back in silence. Each memory from the hospital and the temple flashed across her mind, pushing her to rise above her self-inflicted pain, misery and negativity. Suddenly, an epiphany struck her. She had seen the old pictures of how big her family was. Though they had never visited their relatives in town, mom had told her how her uncles were jealous of their brother getting a government job and standing on his feet instead of surviving on his grandfather's wealth. For the first time, she saw the photo in totality. Even in its black and white treatment she could see clearly – three well-built healthy boys, along with a skinny, dark fellow on the side. That was her father!

She jumped at this realisation and asked, "Dad, why did we leave town when grandfather had everything? Why did you –"

He kept his hand on her head, and Meera did not need to know any further. The hand seemed heavy with exhaustion and carried a weight that nobody could understand. Meera understood everything – she had no words for how proud she was of her father. You think superheroes only exist in movies, but the truth is, they are always around us – we just need to look harder.

Meera walked in and saw Ashna sitting on the sofa. Without hesitating, she stepped closer and hugged her. Taken aback with surprise, Ashna didn't know how to react. She had nearly forgotten Meera's embrace as they grew up. Hugs are usually associated with love and affection, but they have other facets too. For Meera it was a huge leap of faith. A leap that broke down the walls of isolation she had created around herself. Meera embraced her trauma. On the other side, astounded by her sister's reaction, Ashna simply caressed her back.

We think beauty is often dazzling, that it is perfect. With time, we understand that beauty is calm, it gives serenity than excitement. Just holding together what you are is more beautiful than pretending what you are not.

#

Meera rested on the balcony on a lounge chair. She watched herself as a stranger, always silent, in the corner of the room, unable to speak up, suppressing her reactions. The acceptance followed with a smile. One drop of essence changes the flavour of water, so does the inception of an idea. The vow, the epiphany, Ashna's words, mother's lies spoken in affection, neighbour's mean words, relative's inconsiderate opinions, classmates teasing, the never-ending comparison – but still the worst is what she thought of herself. Yes, she could place herself in her father's shoes, almost feel her heart cry, to imagine the hardships he might have faced against their rude uncles. The urban myth about why her grandfather didn't ask for dowry, only if he got the prettiest wife for his son, was an act of consolation – parents do what they feel is best for their children. But his father turned down all the world's riches and raged an unsaid war, leaving everything behind and living on his own terms.

This is what she would also do, but in her own way. The gratefulness of being alive with a healthy mind and body flooded through her heart. Looks do matter but what also matters is how you look at yourself. Yes – this is the complete truth, and she finally understood it.

Change Stories – Next Reads

A Gutterful Life

Hindus and Muslims live in harmony across an open gutter (naala) at the edge of the city.

Whether it's the story of Somu and Aklaq – two innocent souls from different religions who stumble into each other on the naala and foster a friendship like no other; Billu and Arif – two budding businessmen trying to make a living – who are subjected to inter-community politics through the tryst of fate; or the community's favourite Chai-Chachu – an old tea-seller with unknown origin but an important story to tell, *A Gutterful Life* brings forth a plethora of sentiments culminating in an emotional climax.

Will Aklaq and Somu's friendship survive the vagaries of communal division? Will Chai-Chachu be able to bridge the gap between Hindus and Muslims across the naala? Will religious propaganda compel people to forget their hardships and sow seeds of division in the illusion of unity?

First Love Many Times

'She is my life; she is my love. What will I do if I fail? True love only happens once in a lifetime.'

Abhi falls head-over-heels in love with Kavya at first sight. They become friends and everything is beautiful as if they were destined to be together. Until the day Abhi confesses his love for her at the Taj Mahal.

Catastrophe befalls and Abhi's dream shatters. Completely heartbroken, Abhi decides to fight for his love one last time, like the ones shown in movies. If successful, life would be beautiful again, else he would have to end his life.

Will Abhi be able to understand the difference between true love and the one displayed on screen? Will he see reason beyond his anguish? Does love truly happen just once?

This short story debates the question about first love and the trials and tribulations one goes through to achieve it.

Flying With Chains

Three friends – Yatin, Taruni, and Kunal – have been joined at the hip since childhood. They live close by, go to the same school, and always hang out at the same rendezvous. As they grow up, their parents become uncomfortable about their closeness and try to keep them apart.

Whether it's Yatin's struggle to clear the civil services examination, Kunal's difficulty in convincing his businessman father to let him pursue physics, or Taruni's rebellion to break free from the shackles of patriarchy, undue expectations from friends and family builds the pressure on this trio.

Will their friendship withstand the test of time or will the demands of society unravel their relationship and lead to mistrust and betrayal? Will they be able to chase their dreams or will they succumb to their inevitable fate?

A Mother By The Window

'A final lesson for her, she thought. A woman's happiness resides outside herself, in places defined by society.'

Neetu, an obedient housewife, devotes all her time and energy to take care of her family. She is diligent and abides by the rules society has laid out for her. Nostalgia of winning a beauty pageant many years ago and regret of marrying early encourages her to try her hand at becoming an influencer on Instagram.

She works hard to achieve her new goal, without disrupting the life she was married into. Her attention eventually gets divided between her dream and family, bringing to light the secret she is harbouring. The secret hurts her image of an "ideal wife" much to her husband's chagrin.

With Neetu's life in turmoil, Rahul takes a stand to save his mother's dream.

Will Neetu realise her true potential and achieve her dream? Are women expected to fulfil only one role at a time, and no other? Does a woman's personal life belong only to her family? Is there any hope for change?

Also by

Kapil Raj

❦

$\mathcal{N}$ow, a national bestseller.

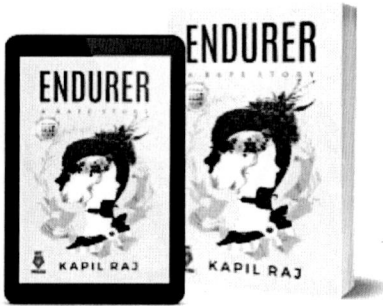

Life was a fun fed roller coaster: new found love, drugs, cat-fights, patch ups, crushes, night hangouts, and unplanned trips. Like any girl, not in the wildest dream, palak could imagine that after attending a rave party, she will wake up to the horror of finding herself raped.

In traumatic conditions and struggle between sanity and hallucinations, she is compelled by the circumstances to leave her world. Already fighting a war within, her stances take a toll witnessing horrifying tales of women and girls. Little did she know that this catastrophe was not enough for one lifetime, and a storm — was just cooling its heels.

Will she be able to carve her path while facing the rapists, her tyrant father, appearances of her passed away mother? Should palak let her life to be decided by people, society, and taboos? Would justice return her life or revenge lend her peace?

A heart-rending story of a girl, whose beliefs and honor has been battered, stands up to make choices, rediscovering the meaning of life.

About the Author

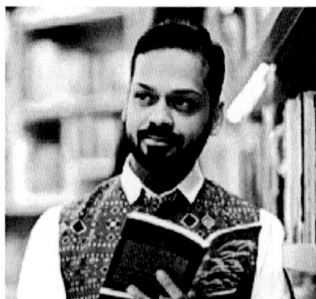

*K*apil Raj is a professional, speaker and writer-activist based in Delhi-NCR, India. With the heart of a philosopher, mind of a realist, and a deep-rooted non-conformist, he lives many lives, yet stealing the time for the most precious thing that matters to him: crafting plots, playing with characters, and weaving the stories based on intricate social subjects and challenging the dogmas.

His debut novel *ENDURER A Rape Story* is critically acclaimed by the media and loved by the readers. He is a noted speaker and delivered lectures in prestigious institutions and colleges.

Connect with him on Facebook, Twitter, Instagram @ikapilraj